Let's Go Visit the School

Originally published as *Barney & Baby Bop Go to School*

ISBN-13: 978-0-545-01715-2
ISBN-10: 0-545-01715-7

10 9 8 7 6 5 4 3   08 09 10 11

Printed in the U.S.A.

First printing, August 2007

Barney™

Let's Go Visit the School

Written by Mark S. Bernthal
Photography by Dennis Full

SCHOLASTIC INC.

New York Toronto London Auckland Sydney
Mexico City New Delhi Hong Kong Buenos Aires

Baby Bop is so excited. She is visiting school.
"Have fun!" says Barney. "I'll pick you up after school."

A friend shows Baby Bop a special place to put her yellow blankey.

Beep! Beep! Here comes the car.

Scamper is a soft and cuddly guinea pig.
He loves to eat crunchy carrots.

Baby Bop makes a sand castle . . .

At story time, the teacher reads Baby Bop's favorite book.

It's fun to imagine being a doctor . . .

Don't forget to wash and dry your hands before eating your snack.

Wheeeee! Baby Bop rides her tricycle on the playground.

Here comes the ball! Catch it!

"See the picture I painted?" asks Baby Bop.
"It's super-dee-duper!" says Barney.